SONG LEE AND THE LEECH MAN

"Harry's in the pond!" *Dexter screamed.*

Miss Mackle leaned over and grabbed Harry's hand. After she helped Harry stand up, we could see the pond was just knee deep.

Harry waded out of the water.

"I'm okay," he grumbled.

Then we stared at him.

There were little jiggling snakes all over his arms.

"Leeches!" Sidney screamed.

"Eeyew!" we all shrieked.

Mary read from the guidebook, "Leeches are aquatic blood-sucking or carnivorous worms."

"Help!" Harry yelled. "THEY'RE SUCKING MY BLOOD!"

"A welcome addition."   —*School Library Journal*

PUFFIN BOOKS ABOUT ROOM 2B

Horrible Harry and the Ant Invasion
Horrible Harry and the Christmas Surprise
Horrible Harry and the Green Slime
Horrible Harry and the Kickball Wedding
Horrible Harry in Room 2B
Horrible Harry's Secret
Song Lee and the Hamster Hunt
Song Lee and the Leech Man
Song Lee in Room 2B

SONG LEE AND THE LEECH MAN

BY SUZY KLINE

Pictures by Frank Remkiewicz

PUFFIN BOOKS

PUFFIN BOOKS
Published by the Penguin Group
Penguin Books USA Inc., 375 Hudson Street, New York, New York 10014, U.S.A.
Penguin Books Ltd, 27 Wrights Lane, London W8 5TZ, England
Penguin Books Australia Ltd, Ringwood, Victoria, Australia
Penguin Books Canada Ltd, 10 Alcorn Avenue, Toronto, Ontario, Canada M4V 3B2
Penguin Books (N.Z.) Ltd, 182-190 Wairau Road, Auckland 10, New Zealand

Penguin Books Ltd, Registered Offices: Harmondsworth, Middlesex, England

First published in the United States of America by Viking,
a division of Penguin Books USA Inc., 1995
Published in Puffin Books, 1997

7 9 10 8 6

Text copyright © Suzy Kline, 1995
Illustrations copyright © Frank Remkiewicz, 1995
All rights reserved

THE LIBRARY OF CONGRESS HAS CATALOGED THE VIKING EDITION AS FOLLOWS:
Kline, Suzy.
Song Lee and the Leech Man / by Suzy Kline; pictures by Frank Remkiewicz.
p. cm.
Summary: Harry plots revenge against Sidney, the class tattletale, when Miss
Mackle's second graders go on a field trip to the pond.
ISBN 0-670-85848-X
[1. Schools—Fiction. 2. School field trips—Fiction. 3. Pond animals—Fiction.
4. Korean-Americans—Fiction.] I. Remkiewicz, Frank, ill. II. Title. PZ7.K6797Sk
1995 [Fic]—dc20 94-39231 CIP AC

Puffin Books ISBN 0-14-037255-5

Printed in the United States of America

RL: 2.1

Acknowledgments:

Special appreciation to David L. Wagner, Ph.D., Associate Professor of Ecology and Evolutionary Biology at the University of Connecticut at Storrs, and his "A Fascination with Insects" workshop at the University of Connecticut Natural History Museum.

To my husband, Rufus, who went with me on the insect field trip and who suggested the title.

And to Jane Seiter, my editor, for helping me with this manuscript.

Dedicated with love to my students, who enjoy fascinating facts about insects:

Sean Baker
Randi Bartles
Chris BeBault
Jennifer Bunnell
Alan Cappelletti
Joshua Decker
Anthony Drake
Casey Fraser
Jamie Gagnon
David Jasmin
Stephanie Jelinek
David Kirschner
Megan Lenart
Angela Marchetti
Torrie Musselman
James Neshko
Corey Pelcher
Michael Pilbin
Sara Roberts
Eric Ross
Derek Shepard
David Simmons
Jessica Smith
Stacey Villone
Brenda Williams

SONG LEE AND
THE LEECH MAN

Contents

Ant Stickers   1

Sidney's Beef   13

Monarchs, Mexico, and
   Spittlebugs   25

The Leech Man!   38

Ant Stickers

I'm worried about Harry.

Next Monday, Room 2B is going on a field trip to a pond. It's going to be the best day in second grade. The teacher said she's leaving Harry behind.

Unless . . .

. . . he can get one more ant sticker on his good-behavior chart.

*   *   *

"No problem, Doug," Harry said.

"I hope not," I replied. "I'll be sitting by myself on the bus if you don't go."

"Harry can be good," Song Lee said.

Harry nodded.

Sidney shook his head. "Today's your *last* chance, Harry. You haven't gotten a sticker in four days. Monday, you pushed and shoved in line. Tuesday, you ran in the hall. Wednesday, you did a karate kick in the library. Thursday, you—"

Harry put his face in front of Sidney's. "*You* should know. *You* told on me."

Sidney continued, "And Thursday, you made silly noises."

"For your information, King Tattletale," Harry replied, "those were not *silly* noises. I was making hornet sounds. We're studying insects. Remember?"

2

"Hornet sounds?" Sidney said. "I thought you were into bird calls, Harry the Canary!"

Harry wiggled his fingers in the air. "You're asking for a tickle attack, Sid the Squid."

Suddenly, Sidney looked like he had a bad toothache. "That's what you did to me the first day of school!"

Miss Mackle drew an ant on the

board. "Who can tell me the three body parts of an insect?"

Song Lee raised her hand. "Head, thorax, and abdomen."

"Good. What else does an insect need?"

"Six legs," Harry blurted out.

Miss Mackle raised her eyebrows. "You forgot to raise your hand, Harry."

Harry sank down in his seat.

"There goes your sticker," Sidney whispered.

Harry waved his hand in the air.

"Yes, Harry?" the teacher said.

"Insects have six legs, four wings, and two antennae."

"Good."

Harry flashed a toothy smile.

Everything was great until we got down to the cafeteria. "Slap me five,

Doug-O," Harry bragged. "We're going on the trip together."

Just as we slapped each other five, Sidney got in line behind us.

"The day's not over yet," he said. "There's still time for you to get in trouble."

"You'd love that, wouldn't you?" Harry said.

"Yeah!" Sidney confessed.

"I thought so," Harry replied. "What's your beef, anyway? Go ahead, spill the beans!"

Beef. Beans. I could tell Harry was hungry.

Sidney gritted his teeth. "I've never liked you since the first day of school."

Harry flashed his white teeth. "All right!" Then he slapped me five again.

As soon as we sat down at Room 2B's lunch table, I started eating. I love pancakes-and-sausage day.

Harry dangled a sausage from his mouth. "Got a light, Sid?"

"I don't smoke," Sidney snapped.

Dexter leaned over and pretended to strike a match. "*Pssssssssst!*" he said.

Mary and Ida started giggling. I did too.

When Harry blew pretend smoke in Sidney's face, I coughed. "Hey, Harry!" I said. "You're polluting the air!"

Song Lee giggled and then popped an orange wedge in her mouth. When she smiled, she looked like a jack o'lantern.

We were having fun being silly.

Suddenly Sidney raised his hand. "Miss Turner!"

The lunch aide came over to our table. "Yes, Sidney?"

"People are playing with their food and *Harry* started it. It was his idea."

Miss Turner frowned. "Are you playing with your food, Harry?"

Harry shook his head.

Then he ate his cigar.

Miss Turner tapped her little red book with a pencil. "Hmmmmm . . . "

Oh no! I thought. What if she wrote Harry's name down in that book? He wouldn't get an ant sticker!

"Harry's lying," Sidney tattled. "I saw him light up that link. He blew sausage smoke in my face."

When Harry started laughing, Miss

Turner opened her red book.

"Wait!" Song Lee said. "I play with food, too."

Miss Turner took off her glasses. "*You* did?"

Song Lee nodded.

"Me, too," Mary added.

"Me, too," Ida said.

"Me, too," Dexter and I repeated.

"Well," Miss Turner said. "It looks like *all* of you are being silly today. Please stop it. Now."

When Miss Turner walked away, she closed her little red book.

Saved! I thought.

Mary shook her carrot stick at Sidney. "You could have gotten us *all* in trouble!"

"It was just supposed to be Harry," Sidney replied.

Mary groaned. "Harry was saved by

Song Lee and his *friends*. Too bad you
don't have any!"

Harry wadded up his napkin and
stuffed it inside his milk carton. "Just
you wait, Sid the Squid! I'll get even
with you. Not today. I can't do it today.
But I can *Monday* . . . on our field
trip!"

And then Harry lowered his voice,
"When you least expect it!"

That afternoon, Harry was a good citizen.

For the next two hours, he raised his hand when he wanted to say something.

He asked permission to sharpen his stub pencil.

He tore out his math page without ripping it.

He finished his subtraction problems.

He drew a giant picture of a black widow and wrote seven facts about poisonous spiders.

At 2:55, Miss Mackle put an ant sticker on Harry's chart.

Everyone clapped . . . except Sidney.

Sidney's Beef

Monday morning, Room 2B lined up for the bus. Today was our field trip!

"Nice hat, Song Lee," I said.

"Thank you, Doug." She had a strainer on her head.

"Going to catch some pond life?"

"I want to bring home tadpoles."

Mary and Ida had butterfly nets.

"*Yahoo!*" Harry cheered. "I'm ready!

I've got three empty containers for *bugs*."

Mary made a face. "You are *not* ready. You aren't properly dressed. You should have your pants tucked inside your socks. Your arms should be covered too. Haven't you heard of deer ticks?"

Harry shrugged. "I love deer ticks."

Sidney giggled. "So why don't you marry one?"

Harry held up a fist. "I haven't forgotten you, Sid. Sometime today I'm getting—"

"Okay, boys and girls, let's board the bus," Miss Mackle said.

Harry whispered the last word of his sentence to Sidney.

I knew what it was.

Revenge.

"Can we sit three in a seat?" Mary asked.

"Either two or three," the teacher said.

Mary, Ida, and Song Lee scooted into a seat together. Harry and I ran for the last seat in the bus. Harry got dibs on the window.

Everyone had a partner, except Sidney.

No one likes to sit next to a tattle-tale.

Miss Mackle put her arm around

him. "Sidney needs to share a seat with someone. Who will that be?"

When nobody's hand went up, Miss Mackle suggested, "How about someone who is sitting three in a seat?"

The bus turned quiet.

Song Lee slowly raised her hand. "I'll be his partner."

Mary made a face. "Song Lee! You don't want to sit with *him*. We want you to be with us."

Song Lee got up and shrugged. "We have lunch together, Mary. Sidney needs partner now."

Miss Mackle patted Song Lee's shoulder. "You're so kind."

Song Lee smiled. Then she walked to the back of the bus with Sidney. They sat in the empty seat in front of us.

I wondered if Harry was going to get his revenge in the bus.

As we drove out of town, it didn't seem like it. Harry didn't say boo to Sidney. He was watching for big Mack trucks. Harry loves to make the trucker honk his big horn.

Since Harry was hogging the window, there wasn't much for me to do. I decided to lean forward and spy on Song Lee and Sidney. At first they were just talking.

"Want to play a game, Sidney?"

"Sure, Song Lee."

"I give you tiny piece of paper and you write down a wish. I write a wish, too. Then we crumple paper into small ball and toss it up to the ceiling. If we can catch paper ball when it falls back down, the wish comes true."

I watched Sidney and Song Lee write on the tiny yellow pads that Song Lee had packed in her bag. I wanted to

write a wish, too. I would wish I could
sit next to the window.

"HONK!" Harry yelled.

When he made his arm go up and
down, he hit me in the head.

"Hey!"

"Sorry, pal."

When Harry looked out the window
again, I looked back at Sidney and Song

Lee. They each had a tiny yellow ball of paper.

"We count to three," Song Lee said.

"One, two, *three*!"

Up went the bits of paper.

Sidney's hit the ceiling. Song Lee's drifted up and out the top half of the bus window.

"Oh no!" Song Lee said, covering her face. "I litter!"

Sidney looked out the window. Then he looked around. "Hey, where did mine go?"

Song Lee took her hands away from her face. "I don't see it."

"Me either," Sidney groaned.

I looked down at the tiny ball of yellow paper that had landed on my sneaker. Aha! No one knew but me. Slowly I picked it up and unwrapped it.

The writing was sloppy so I knew it

was Sidney's. Quickly, I read it.

I Wish I Had a Fred

Fred?

What was that?

Then I wondered what Song Lee wished for. After I thought about it for a while, I put the yellow ball of paper in my shirt pocket and spied some more.

"Song Lee?"

"Yes, Sidney."

"Do you want to know what my beef is with Harry?"

"Do you want to tell me?"

"Yes."

Sidney suddenly turned around to see what Harry was doing. I acted like

20

I was looking out the window, too.

"HONK!" I said.

Harry and I pulled our arms down together.

When Sidney was convinced we were busy, he turned back. And I leaned forward again.

"Do you remember the horrible thing Harry did to me on the first day of second grade?"

Song Lee shook her head.

Sidney continued, "He pinned me down on the ground, and tickled my armpits, and made me say 'I love girls' three times."

Song Lee covered her mouth. She was trying not to giggle.

"It isn't funny," Sidney said. "You know what it's like to be tickled by Harry?"

Song Lee shook her head slowly.

"It's like getting knuckle noogies dug in your armpits. And you and Mary and Ida heard. That was the worst part."

"I forget," Song Lee said. "You should too. It is long time ago."

"I do sometimes," Sidney said. "But when Harry brings up a tickle attack, I remember that day. I can't help it."

Song Lee thought about it. "I remember now. You call Harry canary.

And that started fight."

"But I was just teasing," Sidney said. "I like rhymes."

"Do you like Sid the Squid?" Song Lee asked. "That is a rhyme."

Sidney sank down in his seat. "No."

"Maybe someday you and Harry will get along." Song Lee opened her bag again. "Want to play second game?"

Sidney nodded. "Will *you* be my friend?"

Song Lee looked at Sidney and smiled. "Yes, Sidney, I will be your friend."

I leaned back in my seat and reached in my shirt pocket. Now I knew what Sidney had wished for when he wrote the word "Fred."

Suddenly a big Mack blasted its horn.

"HONK!"

Everyone in the bus cheered and waved at the truck driver.

"Finally, we made progress!" Harry said as he slapped me five.

Yeah, I thought. And so did Sidney.

He finally made a friend.

Monarchs, Mexico, and Spittlebugs

An hour later, our bus arrived at the University of Connecticut.

"Look! There's a cow!" Song Lee said.

"*Moooooo!*" Harry mooed.

"Miss Mackle," I asked, "how come they have cows on the campus?"

"UConn has an agriculture school. Students can learn about plants and animals."

"And *insects!*" Harry yelled.

We all clapped and cheered.

Then Miss Mackle pointed to some brick buildings. "See the dormitories? That's where students live."

When we turned onto the campus, we saw lots of students walking to class. Some were riding bikes.

"I think I'll go to UConn when I go to college," Mary said.

"Where's the pond?" Harry yelled.

The bus parked in front of a big science building. "We have to walk to it. Take your backpacks and lunches."

"Yahoo!" Harry screamed in my ear. *"It's bug time,* and . . ."

Then he tapped Sidney on the shoulder. " . . . when you least expect it . . . REVENGE, King Tattle-tale!"

Sidney moved Harry's hand away. "Cut it out, Harry the—"

When Sid looked at Song Lee, he stopped. The guy was trying.

"Follow me, boys and girls," Miss Mackle called.

We got off the bus and followed the teacher to a big tree across the street.

A man in shorts with a big butterfly net was waiting for us. He had a large rectangular pan under his arm.

Miss Mackle shook his hand. "Boys and girls, this is Professor Guo. He teaches entomology at the university. Entomology is the study of insects."

"*All right!*" Harry yelled.

"So, where are the insects?" Mary asked.

"Everywhere!" Professor Guo said. "On plants, in trees, under just about every rock, near water, in water . . . Two thirds of all animals are insects."

"Whoa!" I said.

Professor Guo pointed to the nearby cemetery. "Let's walk through here. The pond is on the other side. Keep your eyes open. If you see something, tell me and we'll talk about it."

"Uh oh," Sidney moaned. "We have to walk over dead bodies."

Harry smiled. "Neato!"

Song Lee ran after a butterfly. When it landed on a tombstone, she caught it with her bare hands.

"What did you catch?" Professor Guo asked.

Song Lee showed him.

"You're holding it carefully. Good."

Song Lee smiled. "I don't want to

hurt butterfly."

"You know—" the professor looked at her name tag— "Song Lee, there is a Chinese proverb that says all knowledge begins with a name. It's important to learn them."

When he said that, I thought about Harry the Canary and Sid the Squid. Those names spelled trouble.

Professor Guo held up the butterfly so we could see. "Anyone know what the name of this kind is?"

"Monarch," I said.

"Good, Doug. Do you know where all the monarchs east of the Rockies fly to?"

We shook our heads.

"A grove of trees in central Mexico."

"Mexico?" I replied. "That's far away."

"It is," Professor Guo said. "That's why it usually takes several generations to get there. Our New England monarchs might make it to Pennsylvania. Then their children head for Texas. The grandchildren are usually the ones who make it from Texas to Mexico."

"Wow!" I said. "How do they find their way?"

"Their genes probably carry all the map information."

"Jeans?" we said.

"Not the kind you wear," Professor Guo explained. "The kind you inherit. The kind that decide if you will have black hair or blond hair, or blue eyes or brown eyes."

We watched Professor Guo let the butterfly go.

"Keep watching for insects," he said as we left the cemetery and walked across a meadow.

"Look!" Harry called. "I caught a

wasp."

He ran over to Professor Guo with his plastic jar. "Is it a boy or girl?" Harry asked. "I'm not keeping it if it's a girl."

Mary stuck her tongue out at Harry.

"That's easy," the professor said. "Ants, wasps, and bees are mainly female. The females are the ones who get the food. The males generally stay back at the hive or nest."

Mary nodded. "My dad's like that. Mom says he's a couch potato. He just stays at home."

Harry groaned as he let the wasp go. "What about those monarch butterflies?"

"Butterflies are different," Professor Guo said. "They're about fifty-fifty male and female."

"*Yes!*" Harry said, making his arm go up and down. "The males go to Mexico too!" Then he cleared his throat as he looked at a plant.

"*Eeyew!*" Sidney said. "Harry just spit!"

We all turned and looked at the froth on the leaf.

Professor Guo laughed. "That wasn't Harry. That's just a spittlebug building a house of bubbles."

"*Fooled* yah, Sid!" Harry cackled.

I shook my head. I wondered if Harry and Sidney would ever make up.

"Harry's bugging me," Sidney tattled. Then he took half an egg from his lunchbox, salted it with a salt shaker, and started eating it.

"Look out," Harry said. "There's a bug on your yolk. And that's no joke."

"AAAAUUUUGH!" Sidney screamed. Everyone jumped.

Professor Guo rushed over. "It's just a ladybug. They're harmless. And helpful. They eat insect pests like aphids."

"I don't like bugs on my food," Sidney complained. When he dropped his egg on the ground, a dozen ants came out from nowhere and started crawling all over it.

"Insects are high in protein," Professor Guo said. "They are used for food in some parts of the world."

Most of us made a face.

"But don't eat butterflies," Professor Guo said. "They taste awful. Smell awful too. That's why most animals leave them alone."

When Sidney saw a butterfly, he held his nose.

Harry rolled his eyes. "You're a wimp,

Sid. I grew up eating ants on a log. I could munch on a crunchy snail right now."

Sidney stomped his foot. *"Harry! You think you're so tough.* One of these days some insect might bug *you."*

Harry cackled. "Never."

The Leech Man!

I don't know how it happened.

But it did.

We were on the path by the pond. Professor Guo had just dipped his large rectangular pan into the pond water and was showing us some living things.

"Here's a devil's darning needle, or dragonfly."

Sidney took a few steps back. I could

tell he didn't like the name of that
insect.

"There's a tadpole!" Mary said.

"May I have one, Professor Guo?"

Song Lee asked. "I brought plastic container."

"I'm sure you would take good care of it, Song Lee. But let's leave the animal life in the pond. It's their natural habitat. We're here to watch."

When a bumblebee landed on the edge of the pan, we all leaned back.

"Have you ever gotten stung?" I asked.

"Sure have, Doug. It was only a one, though, on the Relative Pain Index."

"What's that?"

"Well, a scientist named Justin O. Schmidt made up a pain index. He went out and got bitten by all kinds of insects. Then he charted their sting—how much it hurt and how long it lasted."

"On purpose?" Mary asked.

"On purpose. It was part of his field work. The highest level of pain is a four. The longest sting recorded was from a tropical ant and lasted twenty-four hours."

"Oooooooh," we said.

"Who else gives horrible stings?" Harry asked.

"The Australian bulldog ant, and a spider wasp."

"Neato," Harry replied.

"What's a three on the pain index?" Mary asked.

"Probably hornets, yellow jackets, and paper wasps. I think a honey bee is a two. I have to check the index."

Suddenly Harry blurted out, "We all know what Sidney is. A four. He's a royal pain."

When everybody cracked up, Sidney said, "Funny. So funny, I forgot to laugh."

Professor Guo smiled and then pointed to something in his pan. "See this water boatman? He's another aquatic insect."

Miss Mackle looked up from her Golden guidebook. "Who remembers what an aquatic insect is?"

Mary shouted it out first: "An insect that lives *in* or *on* the water."

In the next few minutes, while we watched dragonflies, damselflies, and water boatmen dance on the water, Harry moved to the back of the group. I wondered where he was going, so I turned to look.

Harry sneaked up behind Sidney and tapped him on the shoulder. Sid was looking at the pond. When he turned around, Harry wiggled his fingers. "Time for *revenge*, King Tattletale!"

Sidney started shaking. When he took a step back, Harry took a step forward right to the edge of the pond.

And then it happened.

Harry started to give Sidney a knuckle noogie in his armpit. I could tell that Sidney was afraid. His eyes looked like white gumballs, the kind you buy for twenty-five cents in those giant machines.

When Sidney jumped, Harry lunged forward.

Splash!

Miss Mackle dropped her Golden guidebook and rushed over.

Professor Guo set down his pan.

Ida's mother got the first-aid kit.

"*It's Harry!*" I yelled. "He fell in the pond."

"*Harry's in the pond!*" Dexter screamed.

Miss Mackle leaned over and grabbed Harry's hand. After she helped

Harry stand up, we could see the pond
was just knee deep.

Harry waded out of the water.

"I'm okay," he grumbled.

Then we stared at him.

There were little jiggling snakes all
over his arms.

"*Look!*" we shouted.

Miss Mackle's face turned white.
"Professor Guo! What are those snake-

like things on Harry?"

"Leeches."

"*Leeches!*" Sidney screamed.

"*Eeyew!*" we all shrieked.

Mary read from the teacher's Golden guidebook, "Leeches are aquatic blood-sucking or carnivorous worms."

"*Help!*" Harry yelled. "THEY'RE SUCKING MY BLOOD!"

"Now st-stay calm," Miss Mackle said. "We'll get them off, Harry."

Ida hugged her mother.

Sidney pulled his jacket over his head.

Professor Guo asked, "Does anyone have any salt?"

No one said anything. We just stood there. Staring. And cringing.

At . . . the Leech Man!

Professor Guo and the teacher tried to pull the leeches off, but they

wouldn't budge.

Song Lee ran over to Sidney. "You had salt shaker. Where is it?"

Sidney was shaking under his jacket.

Song Lee pulled the jacket off his face. "Your salt shaker, Sidney?"

"Oh! In . . . muh-muh-my ba-ba-bag."

Song Lee reached inside and pulled it out. "Here, Professor Guo."

Everyone watched the professor pour salt over the leeches on Harry's arms.

Harry was shaking and sobbing.

I watched one leech shrivel up in the salt and fall off.

Eeyew! I thought.

"It's working!" Harry yelled.

Professor Guo kept pouring salt on Harry's leeches. Finally the shaker was empty.

"They're gone!" Harry shouted.

Mary closed the teacher's book.

Ida stopped hugging her mother.

Sidney took his jacket off his head.

"Wait, there's one more!" Mary yelled. *"On Harry's neck!"*

Miss Mackle reached over and tried to pull it off.

Ida's mother tried to pull it off.

Professor Guo tried.

Song Lee reached in her backpack. "Wait! I have small bottle of soy sauce. That has salt in it. I try."

Everyone watched Song Lee dump
the plastic container of soy sauce on
Harry's neck.

The dark brown juice flowed over the
leech, and then it started to shrivel up.

Professor Guo flicked it off. "All right,
Song Lee!"

Everyone cheered.

Harry kissed Song Lee on the cheek.

Miss Mackle brought out a light

blanket from her tote bag and wrapped Harry in it. "Are you okay?"

"I'm fine. Thanks to Song Lee."

"Boys and girls," Miss Mackle said, "*please* be careful when you're near the water."

We all stared at Harry. Pond water was dripping from his hair.

"How did you fall in, anyway?" Mary asked.

Harry looked over at Sidney.

One word from King Tattletale and Harry would be in *hot water*.

When Sidney didn't say anything, Harry shrugged. "I tripped on Sidney's bag, and did a flying double somersault into the pond."

That was good, I thought.

"Double somersault?" Professor Guo said. "That would get you in there. Anyway, we were lucky Song Lee remembered Sidney had salt. Leeches are very hard to pull off."

"When we get back to school," Miss Mackle said, "I'll be sure to add salt to our first-aid kit."

Professor Guo smiled at Song Lee. "What were you going to put the soy sauce on?"

"Mother packed me some pulgogi in a plastic container."

"Pulgogi?"

"It is a Korean beef dish," Song Lee explained.

"Sounds delicious!"

"Speaking of food," Miss Mackle said, "why don't we all have our picnic lunches now?"

"*Yay!*" everyone cheered.

Then Miss Mackle added, "Would you find us a nice spot, Professor Guo— that's not near the water?"

That afternoon on the bus ride home,
Harry tapped Sidney on the shoulder.

Sidney turned around.

Song Lee did too.

"Thanks, Sidney," Harry said.

Sidney shrugged.

Then Harry added, "I'm . . . I'm sorry
I acted like a jerk."

Sidney put out his hand.

When the Leech Man shook it, Song

Lee got the biggest smile.

I bet I know what she wished for on her tiny piece of yellow paper.